The Truest Heart

Written by Jayne Sbarboro   Illustrated by Wendy Leach

The Truest Heart

ISBN hardcover 978-0-99-92420-0-1
ISBN trade paperback 978-0-99-92420-1-8

Library of Congress catalogue number 2018903576
  1. Bullying. 2. Kindness 3. Self-Esteem 4. Emotion/Feelings

Cover design and illustrations by Wendy Leach
Book Layout by Andrea Costantine

First printing 2018

Montgomery Publishing Company
Denver, Colorado 80210
www.montgomerypublishingcompany.com

MONTGOMERY
PUBLISHING COMPANY

Dedicated to all who have been bullied
and, with gratitude, to all who will help them.

Ze had a great big heart.

Inside it were many people that she loved.

She loved her mom.

She loved her brother.

She loved her cousin.

And they loved her!

There were so many things that Ze loved.

She loved soccer.

She loved art. She loved math.

And she was getting better!

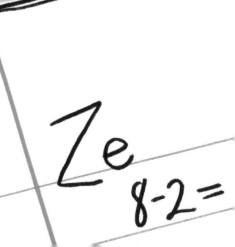

And then there was Jericka.
Jericka did not love her.
Jericka did not always like her.
When Jericka felt mean,
she liked to say that Ze
was not good at
ANY thing.

One day Jericka said the worst thing ever.
Jericka said it loud, and
Jericka said it mean.

Maybe if she had said it in a normal tone of voice,
it wouldn't have hurt.

But Jericka didn't.
Jericka sneered as mean as she could.

And Ze cried.

Ze was lying on the carpet at school.

"What's wrong with Ze?"

"Ze is crying."

. . . And Ze sobbed.

Miss Work took Ze by the hand.

Miss Work said, "Look," and she started to draw.

"Are you good at running?"

Ze knew she was.

She raced every day.

Miss Work said,

"Are you good at art?"

Ze knew she was creative.

She mixed her colors into

beautiful

. . . and she knew when

to color outside the lines.

Miss Work asked, "Are you good to your friends?"

Ze knew she was.

She was loyal to them.

When they laughed together it felt good.

Miss Work drew the outline of Ze on a piece
of paper. She drew Ze standing up. She outlined
a big heart right in the middle of Ze's chest.

She said, "Sometimes people say things
to hurt you."

Ze cried harder.
Ze thought of her friend—
who was not her friend . . .
Who was nice—
who was not nice now.
. . . Who said mean words.

That arrow had sliced deep
into her heart.

Ze was still bleeding friendship.

Miss Work said,

"Just because someone is trying to hurt you,

doesn't mean you let them."

And she said,

"Life hurts our feelings sometimes.

Life does that so our hearts grow.

Without some pain, our hearts

would stay the same size."

Miss Work took another sheet of paper.

She cut out a heart.

It was a true heart, and she began to write.

"My mom loves me."

She added,

"I'm good at being a friend."

She wrote,

"I know I am creative."

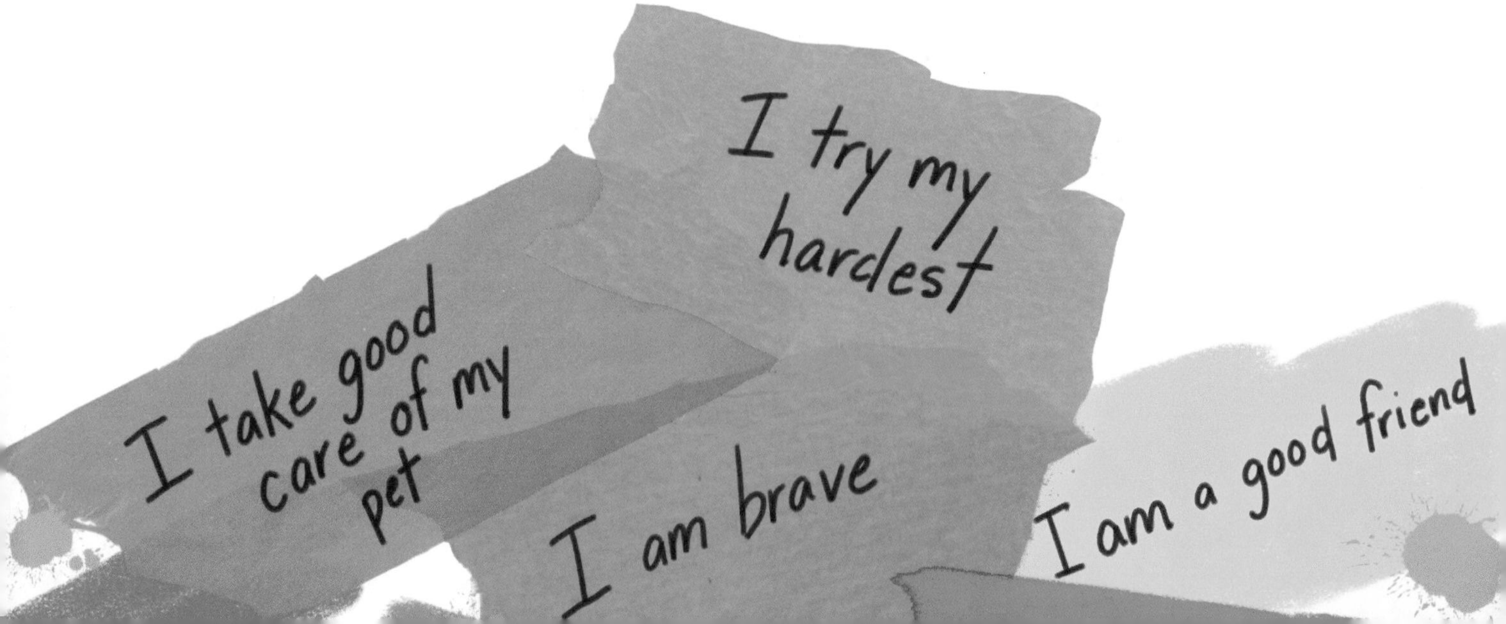

I try my
hardest

I take good
care of my
pet

I am brave

I am a good friend

Miss Work kept writing.

"All these people who love you

     make your truest heart strong.

All those that you love

     make your truest heart brave.

When you keep trying,

     you make your truest heart more dependable."

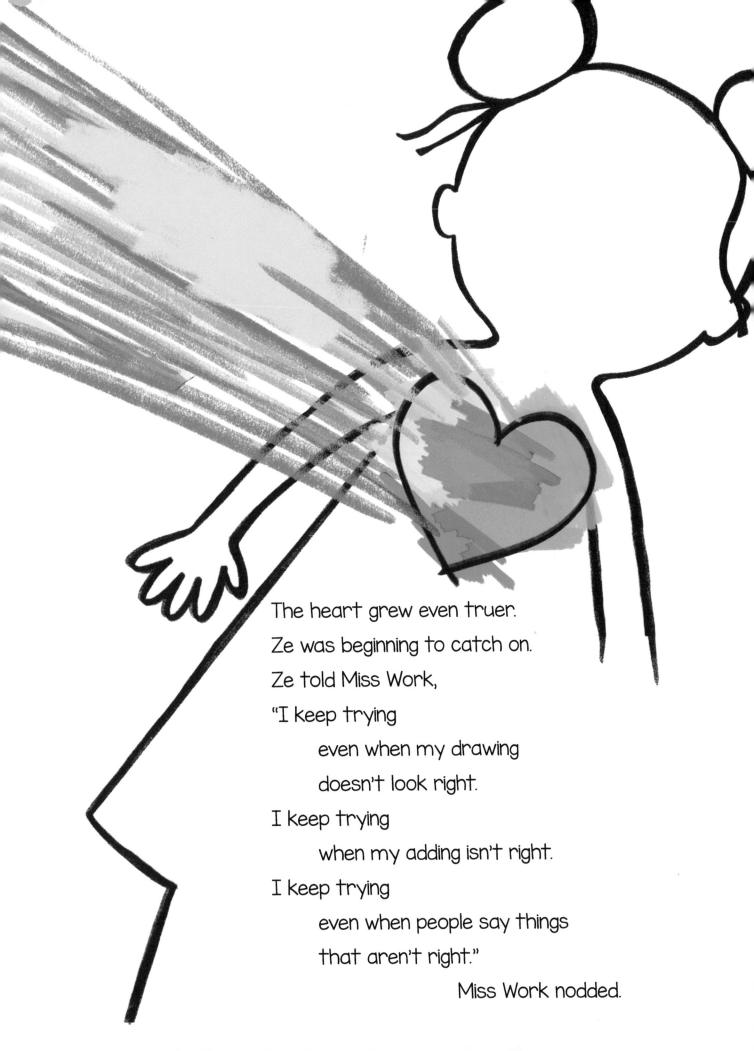

The heart grew even truer.

Ze was beginning to catch on.

Ze told Miss Work,

"I keep trying

even when my drawing

doesn't look right.

I keep trying

when my adding isn't right.

I keep trying

even when people say things

that aren't right."

Miss Work nodded.

The heart the teacher drew was starting to get crowded with colors.

The heart the teacher drew was starting to be full of IDEAS.

The heart the teacher drew was starting to be very full of **good.**

I know how to share

My mom
loves me

I know
how to read

I know I am
creative

"Do you see this heart?"
Ze thought it was wonderful.
Miss Work told Ze,
"This is YOUR heart.
. . . Your **truest** heart.
Wrap your sadness with it.
It will help you feel better.

Miss Work said,

"We practice courage to make our hearts brave.

We use creativity to make sure our hearts stay flexible.

We practice kindness because it keeps

our hearts open to friendship."

Those mean arrows bounced off of Ze . . .

The truest heart
held strong!

And just like magic,
        the truest heart
            was in Ze's heart.
Ze used it each time she needed it.

She made it stronger by loving others.
She made it stronger by being a good friend.
She made it even stronger by always trying her hardest.

. . . Ze knew there would be times when she
would need it to be really, really strong.

And then one day, Angie was lying on the carpet.

"What's wrong with Angie?"

"Angie is crying . . ."

And Angie sobbed.

Ze took out a piece of paper.

She drew a heart.

Reading Time
Angie is a good friend
Angie always tries her hardest
Angie takes care of Michael really great

Jericka watched as Ze
gave Angie a truest heart.

. . . And that led Jericka
to wonder.

the end

About The Truest Heart

Jayne Sbarboro wrote *The Truest Heart* because she saw the effects of bullying first hand.

As the principal in an elementary school for six years, she tried different ways to solve the problem of bullying. Parents of hurt children sat in her office many, many times saying, "I tell my son, just hit them." She could understand their frustration and pain...and yet she knew this wouldn't solve the problem. She wanted to tell parents that if they "won" a fight, they would actually have won the bully's doubled effort to get them back...that the 'winner' wouldn't know whether that would be with an older brother, a cousin, or even a gun.

Over time—twenty-two years as a teacher, two as an assistant principal dealing with bullying on a daily basis, followed by six as a principal—Jayne came to understand that there would always be bullies. When they were caught, bullies would receive consequences...but bullying is often done undercover, out of sight of teacher or parent. Jayne wanted to protect students. When she had a crying student in her office, she wanted to be able to give them a heart shield to defend themselves. This is where *The Truest Heart* came from, and why it is important.

Jayne would ask questions (such as Miss Work asks in *The Truest Heart*). When she drew them on a heart for the student, it was as though students were holding tangible evidence of their goodness. It built their confidence. They had a new echo to replace the hurtful words.

Later, as a reading intervention teacher, Jayne went to a classroom to pick up her student... and it had happened again. Her small student was lying on the carpet, crying. Aside from breaking Jayne's heart, it made her realize that she needed to write the story of Ze, the story of *The Truest Heart*, so that other caring adults would know how to help.

Out of that effort also comes the *Truest Heart Companion*. The Companion book is the interactive version, a guide for the caring grandparent or parent to use with a child, to lead them in the very important conversation that helps their child identify and access the qualities of their own truest heart. Its pages are the canvas for their unique combination of qualities.

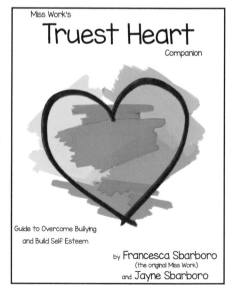

Jayne hopes that Miss Work inspires more children of African American heritage to become teachers.

About the Author

Jayne Sbarboro is an award-winning teacher who has been working with children in elementary schools for the past thirty years. Six years were spent as the principal of an elementary school in Denver where the Truest Heart process was developed. Jayne was a recipient of the Denver Teacher's Award. She was also selected as an American Council of Learned Societies Teacher Fellow to lead a team on inclusive multicultural curriculum. She has been published by the Modern Language Association in *Advocacy in the Classroom: Problems and Possibilities* edited by Patricia Meyer Spacks. She lives and writes in Denver, Colorado.

About the Illustrator

Wendy Leach knew she was going to be an artist the first time she opened a new box of crayons. She knew she was going to be an illustrator the first time she opened *Where The Wild Things Are* by Maurice Sendak. Wendy is a member of the The Society of Children's Book Writers and Illustrators. Her work is showcased at TheArtofWendyLeach.com. *The Truest Heart* is her third book.

CPSIA information can be obtained
at www.ICGtesting.com
Printed in the USA
BVHW021913311019
562620BV00004B/15/P